Welcome
To
Abernathy

J. A. DAWSON

DEDICATION

For my sister.

CONTENTS

ACKNOWLEDGMENTS

I would like to thank all of the friends and family members that took the time to read the various chapters and drafts I sent them. Their constructive criticism and encouragement helped this become more than another abandoned story left in a forgotten folder on my computer.

I
PROLOGUE

Abernathy, New Mexico Territory. Founded by one John J. Abernathy, an illustrious mining tycoon, and passed on to his son, Jeb J. R. Abernathy.

Once a teeming mining town, Abernathy had, in its waning years, fallen into decline; as was the fate of all mining towns. What set Abernathy from most towns of its ilk though was that the mines were still abundant as far as anybody was aware.

The unfortunate truth of the town was that people didn't want to visit somewhere run by Jeb Abernathy, and though his father's reputation was that of firm but fair, this disposition had not passed down to his spoilt offspring. No, Jeb J. R. Abernathy's reputation scared locals into staying and strangers into fleeing.

By the late winter of 1884, only around a dozen men worked the mines; you could call them brave, call them stupid, or call them both: they did it none-the-less.

One December morning, the sleepy town erupted into chaos when the miners returned after an accidental explosion caused part of the mine to collapse. Everybody had escaped out of the mine alive. Everybody except two of the miners, a father and son; in the commotion, the rest of the miners carried the half-charred bodies out.

"What happened?" shouted a member of the town, as they ran to give aid.

"Something — something happened. We dunno!" panicked one miner, as he wiped the mixture of blood, sweat, and dirt from his face, "there — something!"

"What's going on here?" demanded a voice from the crowd. It was Jeb Abernathy; his face half-covered in shaving cream and a flannel tucked around his neck, "what have you done to *my* mine?"

"Mr — Mr Abernathy," stuttered another of the miners, "there were — there was, there, there was a flash of light!

Blue. Green. Both? Filled the mine. Down that area we found that — that cave system? Next thing, ole Jim Sterling and his boy Billy was screaming, then boom! Damn mine started falling down around us."

Jeb pulled the flannel cloth from his neck and clenched it in his fist, "Nobody gets paid until you fix my mine, you hear me? This isn't a holiday; this is a job! Now get back to it!"

Jeb walked away but stopped when a deep voice and heavy footsteps rushed up to him from behind.

"Two of the men just died and you want us to go dig for you again?"

Jeb turned around once more to see Earle Flynt: the head of the miners. Earle's hazel eyes burned bright with flames of seething anger as he stormed towards Mr Abernathy, who tried to remain composed at that moment.

"You boys knew what you were getting into. Mining's a dangerous occupation, and you don't get paid if you don't do said dangerous occupation," replied Jeb, with no concern in his voice as he turned to walk away again, "now, by the sounds of it, it would seem like you boys hit some copper, so, do your damn job! Time is money! Chop chop!"

Earle went to give chase, but two of his comrades held him back and, with a nod, signalled that chasing after Mr Abernathy was not the best idea while the sheriff and his cohorts stood watching with their hands resting on their guns.

"Should've been that son of a bitch dead in the damn mine," Earle muttered to himself.

Many of the townsfolk helped with the two bodies while the rest watched on with tears, and Earle told his men to follow him back to the mine.

"Swear to God, Earle," said one of the younger miners, "that flash came *before* the explosion, not after."

"I know, son, I saw it too," replied a solemn-faced Earle.

The miners dragged themselves back to the mine to start the long and arduous task of clearing it out and making it safe again, but with two of their fellow workers, both of whom they considered their friends, now deceased, morale was at an all-time low.

II
THE OUTLAWS

A lone rider made his way through a mountain pass in Socorro County. With the United States Army still at war with the Apache, and with the Navajo spotted around too, it made for three groups the rider did not wish to meet.

He soon happened upon a small group of men and one woman gathered in the shade under a rocky outcrop.

"He returns!" cried out one man.

The rider sprung from his horse and led it to the other horses owned by the posse.

"Gentile-men!" the rider quipped, "and Janie..." he

continued, acknowledging the female of the group.

"That's a hefty smile. You found something good, Reuben?" asked the leader of the group.

"Sure did, Sam," replied the rider, "there's a town, maybe half a day's ride from here. Looks like it was only just abandoned; like everyone left in an awful big hurry. Everything's just left there, and get this: it has a bank, and I think it may be intact."

"Wonder what spooked an entire town into leaving like that?" asked Janie.

"In these parts? If it ain't one tribe it's the other," perked up Virgil, the eldest of the group.

"More than likely. We all heard that skirmish a few nights ago," replied Sam.

Reuben dusted himself off and sat with the others, "Aye, even I heard it from where I was."

"Well, what do you say, Virgil?" asked Sam, who always

appreciated his oldest friend's wise counsel, "do you think it's worth at least a look?"

Virgil ran his hand along his grizzled face; the bristles on his cheeks and chin gave an audible rustling sound so familiar to the group by now that they seldom noticed anymore, "It's always worth a look, my boy. If it's abandoned, then we needn't worry about the law."

"I guess we only need to worry about a passing company or any Indian scouts that take an interest in an abandoned town," interrupted Janie.

"Well, it ain't nothing we can't handle," chimed another, Clayton, as he polished his revolver with a half-angry, half-joyous grin.

"We should try to avoid a massacre, Clayton," said the last member of the group, Onacona.

"Onacona's right, Clayton," seconded Virgil, "with any luck, should that even happen, we might just talk ourselves out of it."

"You guys never let me have no fun," mocked Clayton,

polishing his revolver with more vigour.

Sam gestured for everybody to gather around him in the shade. Everybody complied and knelt with him as he passed a long-dead and dried piece of branch to Reuben, "Show us, kid, if you'd be so kind."

Reuben took the stick from Sam and drew the layout of the town in the dirt, "Right, we've got Main Street here. From the looks of it, coming in from the south you've got a hotel on the right with a stable behind it. Then, going along that side after the hotel, you've got the sheriff's office, the bank, and a barber, cross the road, and at the end what looks to be a corral."

"Horses?" asked Sam.

"Gone too," replied Reuben, before continuing on, "back onto Main Street, opposite to the corral you got what looks like a bunch of houses, a small cemetery on a hill, and coming back along the road you got a saloon opposite the bank and sheriff's office, then post office, general store, and then a gunsmith."

"Any guns?" asked Clayton, rubbing his fingers into their respective palms.

"Maybe? I didn't get close enough," said Reuben, before continuing to draw out the map of the town, "anyway. Back over here behind the bank, there's a blacksmith, and behind was a chapel. In front of that, across the road, a fancy-looking house; I think the road it sits on leads to a mine, too."

Sam twisted one side of his moustache back and forth between his forefinger and thumb and hummed to himself in deep thought.

"If that bank is empty, then those buildings are sure to have at least a little take; jewellery, weapons, supplies. We can fence any jewellery and take the supplies to head farther west. Get out to California way, with any luck."

"And what if that town is emptier than Clayton's skull?" remarked Janie with a smirk.

"Hey!" growled Clayton before being cut off by Sam.

"Then the only thing we've done is waste a day. No harm done, eh?"

Virgil leaned in to take over the conversation, "I say we

get up first light, eat well, and then head off with the wagon. Sam and Reuben can drive it — if Reuben remembers the way? Onacona can hide in the wagon, just in case the locals have returned. We don't want them getting spooked at the sight of an Indian. Janie, you keep him company, and then Clayton and I will ride up behind y'all."

"Why do I gots to sit in the back of the wagon with Onacona?" protested Janie before turning to her Indian compadre, "no offence, Onacona."

"None taken," replied Onacona, with his stern smile.

"Well, let me think," joked Virgil, "I could either have you ride with Clayton and risk a gunfight between the two of you, or I could have Clayton sit in the back with Onacona and we risk Clayton missing his scalp."

"Ah, come on now, Virgil," chuckled Sam, "they get along just fine, don't y'all?"

"Yes," said Janie.

"Aye," replied Reuben.

"Hmm, ii," uttered Onacona in his mother tongue.

"Sure," answered Clayton, before getting up and walking off, "now, I gotta go take a piss."

Janie leaned in with a menacing grin, "You can see why I wanna shoot him sometimes, can't you?"

"Oh, hush now, Janie," said Sam, with a wry smile, "Clayton has his charms… maybe?"

III
WELCOME TO ABERNATHY

The morning sun painted the sky in pinks, oranges, blues and purples. Its glow brought about a warmth that chased away the icy cold of the night, which the posse had grown accustomed to at this point.

Virgil was, as always, the first to rise. He re-stoked the dwindling fire and began making breakfast. The rest of the gang, one by one, awoke to the smell of beans being cooked. Virgil fancied himself quite the cook and often entertained the idea that had his life taken a less questionable path he'd have made a fine chef in a fancy New York restaurant. He mixed in the last scraps of salted pork they had to hand and had ready the leftover pan de campo he had made the morning before.

"Ding, ding, ding, ding, ding," he said, imitating a service bell as he poured himself a coffee and wore a satisfied grin, "come and get it before the wildlife does!"

Everybody scrambled towards the fire and served themselves an outlaw's banquet.

"Eat till it hurts, gang," commanded Sam, as he shovelled food into his mouth and let the bean sauce drip down his chin, "we've got a big day ahead of us."

The crew continued with breakfast before going about their morning routines behind the privacy of the nearby boulders that dotted the area. By around 10am, they had packed up and were ready to set off towards their hopeful meal ticket of a town. With everyone in their assigned roles, they then set off. Virgil brought along Onacona's horse via the lead and demanded Clayton do the same for Janie's horse.

"I sure hope nobody's picked the town dry in the meantime," Sam said to Reuben on the journey, "maybe we should have left when you returned."

Before Reuben could respond, Janie stuck her head out between them from the confines of the wagon, "Why d'you gotta go say something like that, boss? With our luck as of late, that's the last thing we need!"

"Ha! Now, now, Janie. Were my thoughts premonitions, then the law would have had me hanged many times over," Sam joked, while sporting his charming grin that put anyone at ease.

"Bump," interrupted Reuben.

"Bump?" questioned Janie, before the wagon hit a bump that sent her flying back into the wagon.

"Yeah, bump," repeated Reuben, as he grinned to Sam.

Sam hid his open-mouthed laugh by running his tongue on the undersides of his top row of teeth, before turning his attention back to the dirt road ahead of them. Not too long after, Clayton rode up beside them.

"How far we got to go? My ass is numb and I'm tired of dragging this damn horse with me."

"Not long now," answered Reuben, before pointing, "look. In the distance."

Dancing within in the mirages of the horizon were the

shimmering spectres of buildings and the unmistakable peak of a chapel.

"About damn time!" cried out Clayton, before slowing his horse down to get back behind with Virgil, "we're almost there!"

The crew found themselves in the ghost town by around 4pm, and the sun was already slipping closer towards the horizon. There was an eeriness about how still the entire area was; as if it were a moment in time trapped within a glass jar. If it weren't for the dull hum of the breeze or the occasional buzzard's squawk in the distance, one could suspect that it was a town trapped within an eye-blink.

"Welcome to Abernathy," remarked Clayton, after spotting the town's name on a sign, "population: nary."

Onacona hopped out of the wagon and looked around, "This does not feel right."

"Don't be doing your redskin claptrap here," barked Clayton, "that shit might fly up New England way for the tourists but don't be pulling that mystical 'one with Mother Earth' humbug here."

Onacona glanced at Clayton with a single raised eyebrow.

"No — no, Clayton, he's right," interrupted Sam, "there're no signs of an attack, no signs of something like a cholera outbreak. Hell, no burnt down buildings or anything. It feels like God himself just took everyone up into the Heavens."

He jumped off the wagon and took a walk around it, bumping into Janie and mouthing an apology as she hoisted herself out the back of it.

"Virgil, Reuben, if you'd be so kind as to park the wagon up by the corral and hitch the horses there too. Janie, you check the sheriff's office, Clayton, you check the saloon, Onacona, you're with me; let's go inspect the bank."

The gang agreed to their tasks and set off to their destinations.

"And for God's sake try not to shoot anybody if you find anyone!" cried out Sam, taking the steps up to the bank.

Janie strolled into the sheriff's office with merry abandon, and straight away some familiar faces caught her eye on the noticeboard by the desk.

"Well, I'll be! Who is that pretty li'l thing?" she said, pulling one of the wanted posters off the board, "wanted. Dead or alive. Janie 'Texas Jane' Riley; believed to be a member of the Sam Hyde Gang. Three thousand dollars. Notorious murderer and train rob — train robber? Train robber! I ain't never robbed no damn train!"

Janie then pulled Sam's poster down and inspected it.

"Wanted. Dead or alive. Samuel Hyde. Leader of the Sam Hyde Gang. Ten thou — ten thousand? Hell, Sammy boy, you're lucky I'm on your side because that ten thousand is awful tempting."

Janie continued to pull the wanted posters of her compatriots from the noticeboard until she had the six of them in her hands. She continued to look around as she folded the posters and put them in her satchel.

Meanwhile, Clayton found himself right at home in the empty saloon. After a cursory glance around the room, he made his way to the bar and helped himself to the most expensive drink they had and a cigar from a near-empty cigar box stashed under the counter.

"Gah!" he cried out after taking a swig from the bottle, "cheap bastards watered this down, that's for sure."

He placed the bottle on the bar, not even caring that he almost let it tip over, and made his way upstairs to inspect the room. After seeing that each one was as empty as the last, he put on a content smile and walked across the landing and towards the balcony that overlooked the bank. Clayton lit his cigar and took a big puff from it while watching Reuben and Virgil deal with the horses.

Inside the bank, Sam and Onacona surveyed their surroundings; noting the door at the back but making sure not to miss anything in the room they first entered.

"It looks like people came through here in a hurry," Onacona mumbled, as he picked up a pen from the floor.

"Do you think someone beat us to it?"

"Unlikely. Unless there is a band out there who like to clean up after themselves?"

"Oh, I doubt that very much," replied Sam, as he

signalled to the Cherokee to check the door at the back of the room.

Onacona pointed his revolver into the door and, with a constant push forward, it creaked open. He scanned the room on the other side as more of it became visible to him; a desk, then a vault door, then a second desk, but not much else.

"The room is empty. The vault looks untouched."

Sam grinned and gave out a quick chuckle as he shook Onacona's shoulder in celebration and walked out of the bank to rally the group.

"Guys and gal!" he cried out, "let's do this! Reuben, I need you to crack open the safe. You've got the best ears to listen for the tumblers."

The gang made their way inside the bank. Sam gave the order to Clayton, Janie, and Onacona to keep watch in the front room, while Sam and Virgil waited with bated breath for Reuben to crack the vault's combination. He pressed his ear against the cold metal and began turning the dial, hoping to hear the first tumbler click over the sound of his own heartbeat. The dial rattled as he turned it until: click.

"One down," he mumbled to himself.

As he began the counter-rotation, he stopped short, pulled his head from the door, and listened with close-eyed intent, "You guys hear that?"

"Hear what?" both men asked.

"Sounded like — sounded like screaming, or something, in the distance?"

Sam looked at Virgil, who shook his head and shrugged his shoulders.

"Looks like you're hearing things, kid," Sam answered.

Reuben gave a puzzled look and then continued to turn the dial to set off the second tumbler. After a few moments he heard the click, followed by distant screams again.

"There! I heard it again!" he cried out, "you guys don't hear—"

"What is it, Reuben?"

"I think they're — I think they're coming from inside the vault, Sam," Reuben replied, as the colour drained from his face.

"Ah, shit!" said Sam, before walking into the front room, "looks like we've got a hitch, gang. Reuben thinks he hears people inside the vault."

"So, we leave them in there and rob the rest of the place?" said Clayton, already making his own plans.

"Hey! We only kill who we have to kill. We're outlaws, not assholes!" cried out Sam, "we'll do them the courtesy of saving them first before we rob them."

He then walked back into the room and signalled for Reuben to make the last dial turn. The would-be vault cracker took a deep breath, composed himself, and concentrated on listening for the last tumbler, now through the dial's incessant clicking, his heartbeat, and the muffled screams.

Click.

Sam and Virgil pulled their guns out ready and aimed it at the door as Reuben opened it, allowing the screams to become clearer. The immediate stench of urine and faeces wafted out of the vault.

"Good God! Everything — everything all right in there?" coughed Sam.

In an instant, the screaming stopped and turned into sniffling and quiet, panicked chattering.

"Are you — are you here to save us?" a meek female voice called out.

"Ah, well. Truth be told, ma'am, we're here to rob you, but sure," laughed Sam, as he tried to wave the smell from his face, "we'll save you from choking to death in there first."

The vault went silent.

Sam continued talking, "So, er, why don't you come out with your hands up, slow-like, and while we're emptying your vault, you can explain the predicament that led you to get trapped in here."

"What — what time is it?" asked the voice.

Virgil, humouring the voice, picked the watch out from his pocket and addressed the time.

"Oh, would you look at that? How time flies. It's er — it's coming up to a quarter to five in the evening, my dear," Virgil shouted into the vault.

Quiet sobs emanated from the vault, "You should close us back up and leave before it's too late. Night will be upon us soon, and that's when *they* come."

The three men gave each other an inquisitive look, before Sam asked on behalf of the other two, "Ma'am, who's 'they'? We talking about Apaches or something? Is that who locked you up in here?"

"No, sir," replied the voice, "one of our own put us in here for safety. No, the monsters will be coming."

"Monsters?" exclaimed Sam.

"The dead stopped staying dead here, sir. God has cursed this town!"

"Ma'am, it sounds like you and whoever else in that vault has been in there for a little too long. So why don't you come out, we'll grab you some food and drink, and you can come to your senses a little. How's that sound, hmm?"

Slow and in single file, three women and two children walked out with their hands up, squinting as they adjusted to the light.

"Ah, shit," sighed Sam.

IV
POPULATION: NERY?

Sam dragged two chairs from the desk on his side, and Virgil followed suit with the chairs at his desk. Reuben walked out into the front room to inform the rest of the crew what was happening.

"Ladies, sit, please," Sam said, being more gentleman than outlaw in that moment, "now, what's all this talk of monsters? Did some Apache in war paint come riding through or something?"

Before the woman could answer, Clayton burst in, causing the women and children to jump in abject fear.

"We robbing them or not? Let's go already!" he demanded.

Sam stood erect and his calm demeanour turned sour, "Mr Starr," he said through gritted teeth, "*please* go into the general store and get these poor folk something to eat and drink?"

"I'm no—"

"Now, Mr Starr!" demanded Sam, and as he watched Clayton leave, he barked, "and take the kid with you!" before shaking his head and muttering under his breath, "Jesus Christ."

"We need to leave, sir," interrupted the scared woman, "it won't be long before they're back, and if we're not locked up, then they will get us too."

Virgil, seeing that Sam needed to compose himself, knelt down and reached for the woman's hand, "Madam, we would be grateful if you could make a little more sense than you have been. Could you tell us what happened?"

"You'd think the Devil himself had maddened me for what I'm to tell you," she sighed, "but if we stay around any longer, y'all'll see for yourselves."

"Continue, dear girl. Continue."

"A few days ago, there was an — an incident, an incident in the mine. Two of the men died, and everyone described seeing some flash before the explosion happened that killed them and collapsed part of the mine."

"Sounds like maybe the explosion lit up some copper dust. Those Orientals use it for their fire—"

"I assure you, sir, those miners were mighty convinced they saw the flash *before* the explosion. When Mr Abernathy sent the miners back to clear out the mine, that's when the troubles started."

"Troubles? The *monsters*, yes?" asked Sam, now composed.

"The miners, they, er, they described them as corpses walking around like they didn't know they was dead, and at first it was no problem because they didn't seem to wanna venture out of the mine. So, while everyone was arguing the best way to deal with it, it got dark, and once it got dark, well — well, that's when they came shuffling out from that damn mine."

"And how did you end up in a locked vault?" asked Sam.

"Earle, he — he's the head miner. He, er, he grabbed who he could and locked us in here with some provisions and told us that when everything was clear, he'd come open the door again."

One of the other women spoke up, "We think that was maybe two days ago now."

"What makes you say that?" asked Virgil.

"We figured they only come out at night, and that they knew where we was because we could hear noises through the walls, like they was scratching to get in. It only happened twice, and they felt like they was a day apart each time."

Reuben and Clayton came back into the room carrying opened cans of tinned fruit and condensed milk for the women and children. They grabbed at them with eager hands and acted as if they'd not had sustenance for years.

Sam looked out the window to see daylight dwindling and decided that the safety of the women and children, mad or not, were a higher priority.

"Boys, go back to the store and grab what you can for food and drink. We're leaving."

"But—"

"Just do as I say, damn you!" ordered Sam, before turning to the women and children, "we're gonna take you to — where's the nearest fort to here?"

"I believe Fort Wingate is a day's wagon ride from here, sir."

"Wingate? Do you know the way from here?"

"I believe so, yes."

Sam nodded, stood up, and with one hand gestured that everyone should follow his lead. He walked out the door to see Janie and Onacona standing around awaiting orders.

"Clayton said we're leaving?" questioned Janie.

"The quicker the better," said Sam, "you two go to the gun store and grab everything you can carry, Virgil you go with them. The rest of us will help Mr Starr and Mr Jacobson at the general store."

"Why are we leaving?" continued Janie, as she followed her leader out the door.

"Something ain't right Janie, and I'm not sure we wanna stick around once it gets dark," replied a nervous Sam.

"We not grabbing the money?"

"Our top priority right now is to get provisions and get the hell out of here, second is we get these folks to Fort... Westgate, was it, ma'am?"

"Wingate," corrected the woman.

"Fort Wingate, Janie. We're taking them to Fort Wingate and then we'll come back to finish the job if the Devil himself hasn't dragged this town to Hell."

Everybody then went into their collective stores to grab what provisions they could, racing against the setting sun and with Sam and Virgil both hoping the women were just mad.

"Shh, shh, shh," said Reuben, "do you hear that?"

The group stopped in their tracks to hear a low rumble heading towards them. Sam signalled for everybody to lie low and he walked over to the window, gun in hand, cocked and ready.

"Is that—" he asked himself, before a vision sped past the window and answered his question, "damn it! The horses!"

He burst out the door and saw Janie and Virgil had come out too to investigate the commotion.

"Was that the—" Virgil asked.

"Two of the horses! Did you see which ones?"

Virgil turned to see the annoyed look on Janie's face, "Well, I'm guessing one of them was Miss. Riley's"

"Surprised you didn't recognise your own, Virgil," grunted Janie.

"Wait… damn it!"

"What spooked them?"

"I would ask how they got loose," said Onacona, coming out to join his comrades.

From the far end of the town, the wind carried the horrific sound of the rest of the horses crying out in a series of distressed nays. Sam and Virgil looked at each other with wide and fearful eyes as they both worried that the townswoman's words may have rung true.

"Onacona, stay here," ordered Sam, "Janie, Virgil, follow me."

The Cherokee nodded and watched the three of them slink along Main Street.

"Keep quiet," whispered Sam, "and don't fire unless I say so."

The trio, taking great care to stay quiet, got closer to the corral to see the horses all laying on the ground lifeless and their wagon, covered in sprays of blood, was in disrepair.

"What the—"

"Shh!"

As they got onto the crossroad, Janie looked to her right and, to her surprise, saw a sizeable group of people shuffling away towards the chapel. She grabbed Sam and Virgil by their arms and stopped them.

"Look," she whispered.

"Are they the townsfolk?" asked Virgil.

"Let's — let's back away, slow and quiet-like," replied Sam, "slow. Quiet."

They retraced their steps, being careful as to not alert the large mob in front of them.

"Why they shuffling like that?" asked Janie.

"Shh, I dunno," replied Sam.

"Maybe we should talk to them?" questioned Virgil.

"Oh, I don't think that's too good an idea, now," said Sam, "I don't think that's good at all."

The winds picked up just as they had a few steps to go before the strange mob was out of view. The creatures stopped with a sudden jolt, as if they were one entity, and they sniffed the air like a pack of wolves with a fresh scent in their midsts.

"That — that does not look good," commented Sam.

At once, the mob turned around and looked right at the trio. Their eyes burned with a viridescent hue, as if they were an infernal collection of macabre lanterns.

"Well, fuck me!" exclaimed Janie, as her jaw opened in shock and her instincts made her draw her guns towards the monsters.

"Don't shoot until I say so!" growled Sam.

The pack shuffled towards them, reaching out their hands and howling in a strained and unnatural manner.

"Can we shoot now, boss?" panicked Janie.

"Run and gun!" shouted Sam, as he opened fire on the mob, "back to the bank! Back. To. The. Bank!"

V
THE BEST-LAID PLANS

Sam, Virgil and Janie made their way down the main street back towards the rest of the group, as they took turns taking shots at the horde.

"Why ain't they dying?" Virgil cried out.

"How the hell should I know?" screamed Sam in return.

As they got closer to the bank, and within better earshot of the group, Sam began shouting, "Everybody! Grab what you can and get in the damn bank!"

The women and children, having seen the return of the monsters, let out immediate screams of absolute fear, dropped everything they were carrying, and ran off into the bank. Sam's gang, however, saw the mob chasing after their friends and dropped everything to open fire.

"They ain't dying!" Reuben cried out.

"Shit! I can see that!" shouted Clayton.

"Bank! Bank!" Sam continued to order.

"Damn it! Ona! Let's skedaddle!" barked Clayton as he grabbed Reuben by the shoulder to pull him along to the bank.

Sam, Virgil and Janie weren't too far from the bank when Janie caught a sudden flash out the corner of her eye. She could just about make out the silhouette of a man holding a dimmed lantern at the top of the bell tower of the chapel.

"Hey, I think someone's—" she exclaimed, but as she turned back to tell Sam and Virgil, she misjudged her footing and twisted her ankle.

"Shit! Shit!" she screamed as she hit the floor.

Sam and Virgil rushed back to grab Janie.

"Can you walk?" asked Virgil, as he fired his last shot into the horde.

"I think — ah! Fuck. No. No. Ow!"

"Virgil," said Sam, handing him his second revolver before lifting Janie over his shoulder, "let's go! Let's go!"

The three of them got into the bank and Clayton locked the door behind them.

"Block up the windows and doors best you can boys," ordered Sam, "c'mon Janie, let's get you in the vault."

Sam burst through the door foot first.

"Shit," he said, as he remembered the window in the back office, "Janie, I'm gonna put you in the vault with the other ladies and children then I've got to sort out that window, OK?"

"Who you calling a lady?" grimaced Janie as Sam lowered her onto the floor.

"The wrong lady, it would seem," joked Sam, as he rushed out to tip up a desk and push it against the window.

"Sam!" Janie called out, "Sam! I saw someone in the bell tower."

"Bell tower?" asked one woman in the vault.

"Must be — must be pastor Thomas!" exclaimed another.

Sam returned into the vault, "Whoever it is, they must have climbed up and these things must've not been able to follow... which gives me an idea."

"What's the plan, boss?" asked Janie.

"I'll tell you in a minute," he replied, walking back into the front room.

"We've trapped ourselves! God damn it!" Clayton muttered to himself as he paced back and forth and reloaded his revolvers.

"Not just yet," assured Sam, as he reloaded his gun too, "I got a plan."

"Make it quick, boss!" shouted Reuben, peering through the window, "they're getting closer."

"Janie eyed someone up in the chapel's bell tower. These things must not be able to climb, which gives us an advantage."

"And how we gonna get on top of the roof if these things try to break through?" demanded Clayton.

"We don't," replied Sam, looking out the window, "we get onto the saloon roof instead."

"And do what?"

"Thin the herd."

"Ha! Thin the herd?" echoed Virgil, "Sam, those things weren't falling when we was hitting them."

"Then we keep on hitting them till they do," replied Sam, "so, here's the plan: Virgil, I want you in the vault with the women, children, and Janie. We're gonna lock you in. Rest of us, we're gonna let these freaks get in close and then we'll go out the back window, circle round, go into the saloon and up onto its balcony, climb onto the roof, and then we use all those guns to shoot till they all fall."

"There may be a problem with that," cautioned Onacona.

"Oh?"

"The guns and ammo are still by the stores."

"Well, er—" Sam clicked his tongue with rapid speed against the back of his teeth as he thought for a moment, "er — right, you and Reuben are the youngest. I need the two of you to distract that herd. Make a lot of noise, get them to follow you away to the far end of the street. Clayton and I will grab what we can and get on the roof. We'll let off three shots quick-like when we're up and then you get yourselves back and get onto the roof with us."

Before anybody could argue the plan, the front windows began rattling and squealing as the horde clambered over itself to try get through.

"Shit," blurted Reuben, "they look like they're struggling to get through the glass."

"Right, Virgil, if you'd be so kind as to get in the vault, please?" asked Sam, as he and the rest of the gang backed away from the windows with slow and careful steps.

Virgil nodded, handed Sam his gun back, and walked into the back room to the vault with haste.

"Reuben, go close them in, and then get ready for us to scramble for it," Sam then commanded.

Happy to get away from the impending horde, Reuben chased after Virgil.

"Boys," Sam said in a calm tone, as he reloaded his other gun, "keep yourselves calm, do nothing rash, and, God willing, we'll all leave this alive."

"I don't think God takes a kind view on wanted men, boss," laughed Clayton, pointing his guns at the window closest to him, "same for whatever the hell it is Onacona has."

"Unetlanvhi" informed Onacona.

"Yeah, what Onacona said, Oo-nay-hla-blah-blah-whatever."

"Stupid yonega…" muttered Onacona.

"Shh, shh, shh. Look — listen," interrupted Sam, as he pointed to the windows, "they've stopped."

The three of them stood there, bodies tense, wondering what happened.

"Maybe they lost interest?" whispered Clayton.

"Maybe, yeah — yeah," stuttered Sam, "maybe Reuben was right: they can't get through the—"

"They're coming through!" screamed Clayton, as some glass panes smashed.

"Fuck!" Sam cried out, "make your lead count, boys!"

The trio opened fire at the monsters as they tried to climb in through the broken windows, unaffected by the bullets piercing their bodies or the glass shards slicing through their skin.

"Starting to think that maybe the Devil might be real, boss!" quipped Clayton, as he walked backwards towards the back office.

"Inclined to agree with you, Mr Starr!" Sam cried out, as he continued to shoot.

Onacona continued to fire upon the horde in silence. He stayed still and noted how the monsters reacted as he shot at them. It wasn't long before he had one remaining bullet in the chamber, and he used it to shoot a creature in the head. The light from its eyes dimmed, and the body flopped down over the sill.

"Sam, Clayton. Shoot them in the head," urged Onacona.

"Haha!" cried out Sam, "head means dead! Ha!"

"Great, boss, but I'm running low," retorted Clayton, "I got, er… three beans left in the wheel."

"I am almost out too," seconded Onacona.

"Let's get into the office and—" Sam paused, "Reuben! Does that door got a lock?"

"Let me just — yeah! Yeah, it does!" shouted Reuben from the back office.

"Clayton, Onacona, in the back, go!"

Everyone pushed their way into the next room and Reuben locked the door behind them.

"I don't think it's gonna hold long, boss," suggested Reuben, "it's just a bolt."

"It needn't hold long. When they come through it, we'll — wait, is that vault locked?"

"Yeah, it's locked, boss."

"Good. When they come through the door, we'll leave out this window. Clayton and I will go right, you and Onacona go left and then we follow the plan, OK?"

"OK," repeated the three men.

The door groaned as it was beat upon.

"Get ready to move the desk from the window!" yelled Sam, "get ready! Ready! OK! They're coming through, let's go! Go!"

VI
INSIDE THE VAULT

The women, children, Virgil and Janie sat around a dim lantern in the middle of the vault. They could hear the dulled gunfire cease, and now they knew all that could be done is sit, wait, hope, and ignore the smell.

"Well, this is peachy," sighed Virgil.

"Yeah, bright idea, coming to this shit hole," hissed Janie, as she winced and massaged her ankle with her hand inside her boot, "taken out by my own damn footing."

"We're glad you joined us in here," said one woman, "I fear we may have, well, *y'know*... trapped in here."

"Never know," sneered Janie, "night is still awful young."

Virgil, seeing the fear on the women's faces, tried to change the subject, "So, er, ladies. We apologise for not introducing ourselves. My name is Virgil, and this... *lady*, is Janie."

Janie tensed her jaw and muttered to herself, "I'll give you '*lady*.'"

"I'm Susannah," said the most vocal woman, "this is my sister, Maria, this is Charlotte, and those are Maria's two children, James and Lizzie."

"Well, Susannah, Maria, Charlotte, children," smiled Virgil, "it's a pleasure to make your acquaintance, right, Janie?"

Janie sighed, "Yeah, sure."

"I wish I could say the same," perked up Charlotte, "but I've seen you before. I've seen all of you before. My husband's the sheriff, your posters are on his wall."

"Ah," sighed Virgil, "well, I guess it didn't help that we also admitted we were here to rob y'all."

Janie pulled the folded wanted posters from her satchel and tossed them over to Virgil. He unfolded them and leaned closer to the lantern to read them.

"Heh, you robbed a train?"

"It was news to me too," huffed Janie, rolling her eyes and continuing to rub her ankle.

"Your boss wants to take us to Fort Wingate," continued Charlotte, "they'll hang y'all once we get there, y'know? That's if those beasts don't get to us first."

"*Y'know*," mocked Janie with an angry grin, "they say if a predator chases after you, you don't gotta run fast. All you do is maim the person next to you," she then paused for a moment, "if it comes to it, I'll make sure you're the person next to me."

Charlotte's smugness disappeared, and she shrunk down and kept her mouth shut.

"Is your foot all right?" Maria asked Janie.

"Look, it's bad enough I'm stuck in here with y'all in the first place instead of riding off with a wagon filled with whatever the hell we'd end up taking from here," jabbed Janie, "but can we not make it worse with conversation, OK?"

"She sprained her ankle," quipped Virgil.

"God — God damn it, Virgil!" hissed Janie, as she laid down on the hard floor.

"You should keep it elevated," insisted Susannah, "Mr… Virgil? Be a gentleman and roll up your jacket so she can tuck it under her foot."

"Excuse—"

Janie chuckled, "You heard the lady, Virgil! Give me your jacket so I can elevate my foot already."

Virgil grumbled and chuckled as he slid his jacket off and tossed it over to Janie with a half-smile.

"Not even gonna roll it up for me, eh?"

"You sprained your ankle, Janie, you didn't break your hands."

"Touché, ole pod."

Janie rolled up the jacket, tucked it under her foot, laid back down and covered her face with her hat. Virgil continued to peruse the wanted posters, leaving the women and children to entertain themselves.

Though Virgil lost himself in the posters, Janie kept her eyes open under the hat, and listened to the women talk amongst themselves while playing pat-a-cake with Maria's two young children.

"What do you think will happen if this gang gets us out of here?" whispered Maria.

"With any luck, the army'll shoot them and then take us to Albuquerque," replied Charlotte.

"Not if I shoot you first," chided Janie.

"Y'know, you don't act very ladylike," Charlotte sneered, "'*Texas Jane.*'"

"Well, it's what keeps me alive out there. Don't have the luxury of living in a town... though, if all towns are like this one, that makes me kinda glad."

"What madness caused you to become an outlaw then, huh? Running away from a husband, or perhaps your daddy just didn't raise you right?"

"I'm mighty sure I made it clear I'm not one for conversation," replied Janie, "not with the likes of you, at least."

"And what's wrong with us?" demanded Charlotte.

"Oh, nothing. Just you... lawman's wife that you are," replied Janie, as she shuffled herself to get comfortable.

"Janie, stop antagonising the nice strangers while we're confined inside a locked vault," muttered Virgil, admiring his own wanted poster.

"Fine," she groaned back.

"Who did you kill?" Charlotte then asked, "that's what it said on your poster, didn't it?"

Janie sighed, took her hat from her face, and leaned on her side to face her interrogator, "if I tell you, will you then shut your cock holster?"

All the women gasped, Susannah and Maria covered the children's ears, and Virgil let out a loud, disapproving cough.

"Ugh," sighed Janie, "if I tell you, will you then stop talking?"

"Sure."

"Ladies, you may wanna keep their ears covered."

Susannah and Maria continued to cup their hands over the children's ears.

Janie sat up and placed her hat back on her head, "I had a sister. A little sister who was beautiful, and innocent, and everything I ain't. When our parents were alive, she was the favourite, and I was the rebel. She enjoyed picking flowers in the wild, I enjoyed hunting in the wild. When consumption took ma and pa, and it was up to me to look after her."

Charlotte leaned in and continued to listen.

"One day, I was out hunting, and when I returned, I came home to find a group of men leaving the cabin. They didn't see me. They left damn quick, and I rushed into our little home and — and there she was," Janie paused and took a deep breath, "my beautiful little sister; her dress covered in blood where they — well, I'm sure you can imagine. She was a virgin, and she lay there, staring at the ceiling, sobbing in pain. Her blonde hair was always impeccable. It got dirtied from the struggle and the blood from her neck where they held a knife to it."

"I'm — I'm so sorry," uttered Charlotte, as she placed her hand over her mouth, "you don't have to—"

"No! You shut up and you listen!" yelled Janie.

She composed herself and continued on with the story, "I held her hand, looked her in the eye for a minute, and then I left. I left my sister on the floor and I chased after those sons-of-bitches. I found them taking a piss break, and I walked up to the five of them, gave their legs a quick introduction to my rifling abilities, and while they laid there screaming in pain, I took my hunting knife and one by one I cut their cocks off, stuffed them into their mouths, and let their horses loose. They were still just about alive when I left them."

"Oh my God…"

"I returned home. I remember how cold my hands felt, and opening the door, how quick — how quick I fell to my knees."

"Please, you can stop—"

"My beautiful sister. I wasn't there when she needed me most. She'd, er, she'd sat herself at the dining table and slit her wrists; bled out by the time I got home. She looked — she looked so pale. My beautiful sister."

Tears streamed down the three women's faces, though none more than a very remorseful Charlotte.

"Turns out two of the men were cousins to a local sheriff, and I left a trail. I had only just finished putting my sister in the ground before I had to go on the run. Weren't too long after I met one Mr Sam Hyde and his associate here, Mr Virgil Blake. I was trying to steal food from their camp, but I was so tired and hungry I fainted and fell onto a damn tent. Woke up, and Sam gave me a choice: eat something and fuck off with no harm done or eat something and join him and Virgil. Five years later, here I am, stuck in this shit hole of a vault with a fucked foot telling yarns to yacks."

A single tear rolled down Janie's face, and she went back to laying down with her hat over the face.

Virgil pulled his pocket watch out and squinted at its face, "Christ… we've only been in here twenty minutes."

"Great. Thanks for the update, Virgil," Janie huffed, "thanks a bunch."

VII
OUTSIDE THE VAULT

Reuben and Onacona climbed out the back office's window and hurried off behind the neighbouring buildings to get some distance. They hid around a corner and watched Clayton and Sam make their way out too. Reuben then led Onacona onto the crossroad and they watched the large horde flood into the bank.

"We've got this. We can do this," said Reuben, psyching himself up, "you ready, Ona?"

"Yes, I am ready."

The two began whooping, hollering, waving their arms about; doing anything to gain the pack's attention.

"I don't think it's working," panicked Reuben, trying to come up with an idea, "hang on, I think I've got a bullet or two left."

"Make them count, my friend," encouraged Onacona.

Reuben took a few steps forward, pointed his gun towards the horde, and opened fire. One bullet hit the ground and ricocheted into the leg of one creature, and the other bullet went clean over the horde.

"Your aim is terrible," sighed Onacona.

"My hand is shaking too much!" exclaimed Reuben, "it was all right in the bank at close range."

"Well, it seems to have worked. Look."

The horde began turning in unison and ambled towards the two of them.

"Right, ah, er... shit. Shit. Shit! Shit! Shit, shit, shit! I don't — this is — do we let them mosey over for a bit before we run? Or do we run now?" asked Reuben, shaking even harder with nerves.

"They move slow. Their strength will come from their numbers. We should wait until they are closer," answered Onacona.

"Right, yeah. Right. We'll wait. We'll wait," continued Reuben, "um, Onacona? Do your people have any stories about things like this?"

"We have stories of a creature called the Nun'Yunu'Wi. It is a sorcerer with skin that no weapon can damage, and it eats humans. It uses a magical cane to control the minds of men."

"Do you think these things are, nun — nun-nay — do you think they're those things?"

"Do you see any of them carrying a magical cane?"

"I mean, it's a — it's an enormous crowd. There might be one in the middle of it all?"

Onacona and Reuben looked at each other, looked at the horde, and then looked at each other again.

Reuben walked backwards, "Er… should we—"

"Yes, we should," interrupted Onacona, pointing to more of the creatures coming from the direction of the mine, "look."

Sam and Clayton kept themselves hidden behind a corner of the hotel next to the bank and watched the horde turn and head towards Onacona and Reuben.

"We'll let them get farther down the street and then we'll make a run for those guns," whispered Sam.

"This in insane, boss. This is *fucking* insane!" Clayton said through a gruff whisper.

"I've seen a lot of strange stuff out in the wild in my time, but this… this is echelons above any of that."

"I don't know what an echelon is, boss, but I get the sentiment."

"It's French. I think. Virgil taught — wait, shh, I think they're far enough away for us to sneak over to the guns."

The two men crept in silence across the road towards the gun store.

"We'll grab two rifles each and as much ammo as we can," commanded Sam, "I'll grab rifle cartridges, you get the revolver rounds."

"Got it."

The two of them picked up the rifles left outside the gun store and stuffed as many boxes of ammo into their satchels.

"Try not to rattle them too much," urged Sam.

"I know, I know."

"Satchel's getting full, you got any space left in yours?"

"I can fit… maybe two more boxes."

Sam passed Clayton a box of handgun ammo and the two of them snuck towards the saloon. Sam took great care as he opened the swing door to let Clayton pass through, then guided it back into place as he entered too.

"This way," muttered Clayton.

Sam followed him up the stairs and across the landing towards the saloon's balcony. Clayton handed his boss the two rifles he was carrying and hoisted himself up onto the facade first.

"What's the roof like?" asked Sam, handing the rifles up to Clayton.

"Sloped, but flat enough," he replied, placing the rifles in a pile next to him, "you coming up, boss, or is the view good enough from there?"

"Smart-ass," coughed Sam as he signalled for Clayton to help lift him up.

The duo got themselves settled on the roof and took a moment to calm themselves. Sam grabbed a box of handgun ammo out of his satchel and reloaded his revolvers, keeping three bullets tucked in his hand.

"Right, let's do this," he said, as he aimed up into the air and fired three shots in quick succession.

Reuben and Onacona found themselves by the graveyard on the hill, trying to figure out how best to circumvent the horde.

"I say we run down to the right, through the houses and behind the buildings. Saloon'll have a back door and we can go through that to get ourselves up onto the roof of it," Reuben reckoned.

"I think—" Onacona stammered as they heard the three gunshots Sam promised.

"Go! Go! Go!" shouted Reuben as he grabbed Onacona by the arm and began running.

They ran between the houses, up behind the Main Street buildings, and got themselves close to the saloon.

"We're coming!" Reuben began shouting up to the roof.

Sam's head popped out over the roof, "Great, kid! Get your asses up here, rápido!"

"We're on it!"

Onacona ran ahead after he spotted the back entrance to the saloon. He grabbed the handle and began rattling it, "It is locked!"

"Kick it down!" shouted Reuben as he caught up.

Onacona kicked at the door, "It will not budge!"

"Together, on three," said Reuben, "one. Two. Three, go!"

The two of them began kicking with frantic fury at the door, but it didn't budge. They kept on kicking until they heard gunfire from above.

"Hurry the hell up!" shouted Clayton, leaning over the

edge.

"Fuck this," growled Reuben, noticing the horde getting closer, "c'mon Ona, round the front, go, go!"

The two of them continued to run, going past the general store and gun store before they could get to the front of the saloon. As they slammed through the swing doors and headed towards the stairs, the back door smashed open as the horde tried to break through.

"Oy-yoy-yoy!" Reuben cried out in disbelief as he followed Onacona up the stairs.

They ran across the landing and onto the balcony. Sam and Clayton leant over the facade and each one helped another up.

"C'mon, kid," groaned Sam as he helped lift Reuben.

"Jesus, you're heavier than you look," cried out Clayton as he tried to pull Onacona up.

The four men sat down; exhausted and shaking from

adrenaline, they all burst out in uncontrolled laughter that drowned out the groans of the monsters below them.

"What — what the hell are we doing?" cried out Reuben through the laughter.

"I — I dunno, kid. As bank heists go, this is the worst so far," Sam retorted.

"So, er… what do we do now?" asked Clayton.

"Ain't it obvious? Thin out the herd," laughed Sam, as he got up and looked over the edge to see the horde starting to swell around the saloon, "a whole lotta thinning."

He went to sit back down again, but a light in the distance caught his attention; the same light Janie saw from the chapel's bell tower.

"Psst, Clayton. Hand me that rifle with the scope on."

Clayton handed Sam the rifle, and he aimed it towards the chapel.

"That don't look like no padre," he mumbled to himself.

"Lemme see," said Clayton, grabbing the rifle off of his boss, "looks — looks more like a miner."

VIII
A LONG NIGHT AFTER A LEAD SHOWER

The four men shared the rifle ammo between themselves and then took aim at the heads of the countless monsters that made up the ever-growing horde.

"Now, boys," said Sam, "not saying this is a competition or anything of the sort like that, but I will drop more of these sapheads than any of you."

"Oh, you are on, Sam," declared Clayton, leaning over the edge and opening fire, "you are on!"

"Remember: head means dead, boys!"

The four gang members all took their shots at the horde,

shouting out their tallies with every successful headshot. The noise was deafening as it echoed out across the vastness of the New Mexico landscape, and their ears all rang with a high-pitched hum as the shooting went on.

"There's so goddamn — twenty — many of them!" shouted Clayton.

"Seventeen — What?" Reuben shouted back.

"I said: there's — twenty-one — so goddamn many of them!"

"Eight — You said it! — teen," continued Reuben, still without hearing Clayton with any clarity.

"Seventeen — I hope you're making those—" Sam stopped in excitement, "whoa! Twenty! A-ha!"

Clayton stopped firing and walked over to Sam. He looked over the facade, "Did you just skip three?"

"Yeah, look, I shot that one on top," said Sam, pointing to three bodies piled on the ground, "bullet passed clean through, got the next one, then they slumped into that bottom one and knocked it through the railing and its head smashed open."

"Well, damn me O lord," laughed Clayton, before pulling out one of his revolvers and letting off shots in rapid succession, "twenty-four, five, six, seven and twenty-eight."

Sam raised an eyebrow and gave his comrade a disapproving look, "Go back to your own spot, jackass."

Clayton gave a smug grin and pointed his gun over the edge without looking, then pulled the trigger, "Twenty-nine," he then said, as he laughed and went back to his original spot.

"I think there may be more of these creatures than we have bullets for," cried out Onacona.

"There's gotta be at least a thousand here!" replied Clayton, settling back into his spot.

"What I wanna know is: where did they all — twenty-one — come from?" shouted Sam, "and what happened to the — twenty-two — townsfolk?"

"I think some of these creatures were the townsfolk, Sam," continued Onacona, "look at the ones wearing clothing, some of them look old and some of them look new."

Sam peeked over and noted Onacona's observations. He spotted clothes that looked recent, but also noticed how some clothes were old and ragged with styles that weren't even from the same century, and the most ragged of them all seemed to pre-date even the Founding Fathers' attire.

"What the hell have we stumbled upon?" Sam thought to himself.

Just over an hour had passed, and the men found themselves almost spent of their ammunition. The horde, although sparser now, were still many in number. The four gang members estimated between them they had downed at least five-hundred of the creatures but felt despair at the sight of the hundreds still left.

"Save what we have left, boys. Never know, we might wanna end up using them on ourselves," sighed Sam, as he slumped down on the floor of the roof and emptied his revolver of its spent casings.

"So, what? We just sit up here and wait now?" asked

Clayton, before firing off one last shot, "hundred-and-three."

"Correct," replied Sam.

"Anybody got the time?" asked Reuben.

Onacona looked above at the half-moon's position, "Maybe not even nine yet."

"You've gotta be shitting me," Clayton barked, throwing a handful of spent casings in anger.

"Y'know, thinking about it, one of those women from the vault was saying how the miners found these things down in the mine, and they only came out once it got dark," said Sam, "makes me wonder if they won't head back there once the sun comes up. Maybe — maybe that's, like, their camp or, or, or their lair?"

"Well, I guess we just sit here then for the next nine or ten hours freezing our asses off, and then we'll find out if these pig-ugly fucks shuffle back to the mine or if they stick around waiting for us to make a move of our own," huffed Clayton.

"Right, here's how it's gonna be: I'm taking first watch while you three get some rest. Then Clayton, Onacona, and then you, Reuben. If anything happens on any of your watches, you wake me up, OK?"

"Between the ringing in my ears and the sound those things are making, I'm not sure I'll be getting any rest," muttered Reuben.

"Well, just try, kid," replied Sam, "just try. It's a hell of a night ahead of us, and we're gonna need all the strength we can muster."

IX
THE MORNING AFTER

As planned, over the course of the night, the men took turns keeping guard. Except for Clayton, who could sleep through an entire war, the rest of the men got very little in the way of rest.

Sam felt like he'd only just drifted when a sudden jolt from a quick shove to the arm awoke him. He jumped up and reached for his revolver, but Reuben grabbed a hold of his arm.

"Boss, they're on the move," he whispered to Sam.

"Wake up the sleeping beauties, kid," coughed Sam, as he crawled over to the saloon's facade.

As Sam predicted, the broken-up horde congregated and shuffled as one back in the direction of the mine. The rest of the men joined their boss and watched the unnatural spectacle in cautious silence.

Sam looked up and noticed the horizon starting to shift in colour, "I guess I was right, look, sun's coming up."

"So, what's the plan, boss?" asked Reuben.

"I dunno yet. Let's wait for the sun to come up more and for those things to leave, then we'll climb down and regroup with Virgil and Janie."

They continued to watch the horde drag itself down the street as the sky in front of them got lighter. Sam noticed the silhouette of the man in the bell tower again and waved his hand in acknowledgement. The silhouette returned a wave in kind before disappearing downwards.

"Looks like we've got one more person to save," Sam said to his gang.

"Boss, since when was we in the business of saving folk?" Clayton questioned.

"Since we stumbled into this damn nightmare, Clayton," replied Sam, "thieving's one thing, but what's left of my conscience won't let me let those folk die in this god-forsaken place… not if they turn into *those* things."

"Well, I don't much care for getting turned into one of those things either, Sam, so let's just grab everyone, get everyone to take what they can, and get the hell out of this place."

"I am inclined to agree with Clayton," said Onacona.

"Ha! There's a first," Sam quipped, "but no, no. These things need stopping. You see some of their clothes? Some of them looked centuries old. Maybe these things have been around since the Spanish settled here, hell, maybe longer. I dunno. Either way, it's clear they've been around a long damn time and lord knows what'll happen if these things get out into the wider world. Do y'all wanna get caught between the U.S. army, the Apache, *and* these things? Cause I sure as shit don't."

"What you suggesting then, boss?" grunted Clayton, "we gonna — we gonna go into the mines or something? Smoke the bastards out until there's none left?"

"Pretty much. That mine's gotta have some dynamite lying about. If those things like staying in a group, we can blow them up real easy and seal that mine off."

"That's suicide."

"Well, Clay, if you wanna stay here with the women and children then by all means."

"Don't—"

"What, hmm? Don't what?"

"Don't do that."

"Then trust me, Mr Starr."

Clayton stood up and began pacing, "Onacona's the fastest runner, send him to the fort, get us reinforcements or something, I dunno! Anything's gotta be better than going into a mine filled with them things."

"You want me to send a lone Indian running towards a

U.S. Army fort during a war with an Indian tribe?" Sam retorted.

"Well, he ain't Apache!"

Onacona let out a single laugh, "I do not think they will care, Clayton."

"Boss," interrupted Reuben, "what if I went with Ona? They'd be less hostile if they didn't see him as a threat, right?"

"It's the U.S. Army, kid," replied Sam, "God knows with that lot… and besides, we don't even know where the fort — wait, one of those women does, though."

"What do we do then?"

Sam held his breath and closed his eyes; determined to come up with a plan. He hoped if he ran out of air it would make him think quicker.

"Here's what we're doing," he said through a loud, exhausted exhale, "Clay and I, we're gonna go get our mysterious Quasimodo from that tower. Reuben, you're gonna get the vault open again, and Ona, you're gonna gather up some of that food in the store. Then we'll have breakfast, and then I can explain the rest of the plan."

"Well, it's a start," huffed Clayton.

The men went back to watching the horde as it got to the crossroad. It turned and continued up the road that led back to the mine, racing with a stumbled march against the sunrise that revealed more and more of the carnage left around the saloon.

"Let's climb down, quiet-like, OK?" whispered Sam.

The other three men nodded in agreement, grabbed their rifles, re-holstered their revolvers, and climbed over the facade and descended back down onto the balcony, now covered in a carpet of bodies. They then made their way across the landing, down the stairs, and back onto the street.

"These things smell like cooked eggs," commented Onacona, taking great care to step over the bodies.

"That's one way to describe it," said Clayton, taking less care and walking right over them.

"Clayton, with me," ordered Sam, "you boys be careful. We don't know if there're strays hiding in the buildings."

Onacona turned back towards the general store and Reuben wandered through the bank door.

Sam and Clayton made their way past the bank to the blacksmith behind it, and from there they trudged towards the back end of the chapel as not to catch the horde's attention as it continued on its way.

"Did you hope you'd wake up back at the camp?" whispered Clayton.

"I suspect we all did," replied Sam, "these things is mighty fascinating though, ain't they?"

"Not sure it proves if the Devil's real or if God's not."

"Yeah, it's — OK, they're far enough away I reckon. Let's get into this chapel and find out who this person is."

The two men kept close to the chapel wall as they moved along towards the front door.

"If there's anything in here, we use our knives, Clay," said Sam, "we don't wanna be alerting the freaks."

"Got it."

With nervous anticipation for what could be inside, they opened a door each and darted their eyes around to see if there were any of the creatures. After figuring that the building was empty, they closed the doors behind them and walked over to the far end.

"Watch your step," said Sam, pointing to the fly-covered excrement spread across the floor below the bell tower.

They looked up to see a man looking back down at them.

"Howdy," greeted Sam.

"Howdy," echoed the stranger.

"I'm Mr Hyde, and this here's my associate Mr Starr. We was thinking perhaps you wanted to come down now?"

"If you could prop that ladder back up for me then?" said the man, "I saw what you gone done out there, wasting all them bullets like that."

"Oh, come on now, stranger! I don't think getting rid of a few hundred of those things was a waste," replied Sam, picking up the ladder and placing it against the wall for the man.

"They'll get up again."

"Nah, shooting them in the head stops them dead, stranger. Those things ain't getting up again. We watched the literal light go from their eyes."

"Oh, trust me. I know. But you just wait for the sun to touch them bodies, you'll see."

Sam and Clayton looked at each other, looked out the window to the rising sun, looked at each other again, then ran out the chapel and back the way they came. The two men returned to the street, guns at the ready, and watched with tensed bodies as dawn made its mark on the ground.

Without warning, the bodies of the creatures made hissing noises and all at once deflated and turn into dust. The dust whipped up into the air, as if it were a living entity, and drifted at a steady pace towards the men. All they could do was cover their faces and drop to the floor as the dust passed over them and headed in a straight line back towards the mine.

Sam and Clayton looked dumbfounded as they stood back up and saw piles of clothes and bullet fragments.

"Told you," boomed a voice from behind them.

"Gah! Jesus!" shouted Clayton, jumping away in fear.

"They'll all come back tonight. You might have already seen the naked ones? That's what happens after you kill them," said the man, holding out his hand, "I'm Earle—"

"The man that locked them women and children in the vault?" Sam interrupted.

"Are they all right?"

"Well, we left them in the vault with an old man and an angry woman, so your guess is as good as mine."

"Is that the man from the bell tower?" shouted Onacona as he walked out of the general store, "and what happened to all of the bodies?"

"Yes it is, and fuck knows," answered Clayton.

"Don't matter if these things are dead or alive, they turn to dust when the sunlight hits them and then the dust flies back into the mine," answered Earle.

"Earle, is that you?" cried out Maria from the bank entrance, "oh, my lord!"

Earle ran over to Maria and the other women and children and embraced them all. Virgil and Reuben walked out with Janie limping behind them.

"How's the foot?" asked Sam, walking to meet them.

"I'll survive," said Janie.

"Yeah, you will," replied Sam with a smile, before turning to Virgil, "how you doing, old man?"

"Best night's sleep I've had in a while," Virgil joked.

Sam hugged his friend then signalled for everybody to gather around him, "Folks, I got a plan, but first we're gonna eat breakfast because I am famished!"

X
THIS LITTLE PLAN OF MINE

The gang, Earle, and the women and children sat inside the hotel next to the sheriff's office eating out of the assortment of tin cans Onacona collected from the store.

"So, here's the plan," said Sam between chews, "Reuben and Onacona, you two are gonna take a long run to Fort Wingate, and you're gonna go as soon as possible — I'm sure one of these fine folk can point you in the right direction."

"What do we tell them when we get there?" asked Onacona, "I do not think they will believe a story about a cursed town."

"Well, provided they don't shoot you first, Ona, I guess you tell them there's an Apache attack on the town?"

"The Apache don't come anywhere near here; they avoid it like the plague," interrupted Earle.

"Gee, I wonder why?" retorted Clayton with an exaggerated eye roll.

"Er... I imagine it's a long run so I'm sure you'll think of something," reassured Sam, "next, the rest of us. We get all the food and some weaponry back onto the saloon roof. Those things don't climb and at this point I assume it's a damn sight more preferable to a vault; so, we're gonna put the women and children up there — any of you ladies know how to shoot?"

"My husband is — was the sheriff, he taught me how to shoot," replied Charlotte.

"Well then, ma'am, you're in charge of... protecting the roof," said Sam, "now, Earle, you're a miner, right?"

"Yeah, head miner," answered Earle.

"There dynamite still on site?"

"As far as I'm aware."

"Good. You're coming with the rest of us then. We're gonna go into that mine and end this."

"I ain't going back in that mine, mister. There're hundreds of those things."

"You know the layout of that mine. We don't. You're coming with us and you're helping us destroy that horde of freaks."

Clayton pulled one of his revolvers out and rested it on the table, "Don't make me have to think of something threatening to go along with this gesture."

Earle slumped back in his chair and sighed, "I guess I'm going with you then."

Clayton gave a sarcastic smile and slid his gun back towards himself before rehousing it in its holster.

"Eat till it hurts, folks. We've all got a job to do," declared Sam, stuffing more food in his mouth.

The group spent the next twenty minutes eating in relative silence; the weight of what was to come caused an air of solemn reflection.

Once they had finished eating, everybody gathered outside. Sam and his gang said their goodbyes to Reuben and Onacona.

"Try not to die out there, kid," said Sam, "they'll most likely shoot Ona without you there."

Reuben gave Sam a blank stare, "Thanks, boss. Thanks."

Sam laughed and hugged his youngest gang member, "You'll be fine, Reuben. Just fine."

"Be careful, Sam," said Onacona, shaking his boss' hand.

"And you, unalii," replied Sam.

"Five years and you still pronounce it wrong."

"You can learn it to me proper-like when this is all over," laughed Sam.

Reuben and Onacona continued to say their goodbyes, and after saying goodbye to Janie, Sam pulled her to one side away from everybody else.

"What's up, boss?" she asked.

"I want you on the roof with the women and children."

"No."

"No?"

"I ain't getting stuck up on no roof while four old men try to blow up a mine filled with God's mistakes."

"I can't concentrate on being safe if I'm busy worrying about you, Janie."

"Why the hell you worrying about me?"

"Janie. This gang is my family. I worry about you all," sighed Sam, "even a blind man could see your foot still ain't right. If we need to skedaddle out that mine all quick-like, or if we get trapped, or—"

"Sam. I'm going with y'all," said Janie, ignoring his orders and hobbling back to Virgil and Clayton.

"Texas Jane," Sam muttered to himself, "*Texas pain in my ass.*"

Reuben and Onacona began their run in the direction Earle and Susannah pointed them in, and the rest of the group got on with preparing for the day ahead.

Sam and Virgil grabbed the bedding from the hotel and emptied them of their straw innards before taking them outside; with some of it used to create makeshift bags to help carry things, while the rest of it used for the women and children to keep warm on the roof should they end up stuck there overnight.

Clayton made sure the gang was well stocked with ammunition and gave Earle two revolvers and a box of cartridges.

"We'll be protecting you while you and Sam sort out the dynamite situation," Clayton reassured with his smug grin.

He then made sure there were a few boxes of rifle ammo packed in the makeshift bag for the roof before walking up to Charlotte and handing her the scoped rifle and a handgun.

"You got five beans in the wheel," he whispered to her as he handed her the revolver, "if everything goes to shit, which I suspect it will, you save the last one for yourself."

Charlotte gave Clayton a mortified look, which he returned with a stern look of his own that suggested he wasn't messing around.

After they had readied everything, Sam and Earle helped the women and children onto the saloon's roof, then made their way back to the street. With a last check of everything, the gang readied themselves and, led by Earle, began their journey towards the mine.

"Ma'am, are you gonna be all right with that hobble?" Earle asked Janie.

"Fuck off," she replied with a stern face.

The three gang men chuckled at their comrade's all-too-familiar way with strangers.

"So, Earle," asked Sam, "them kids yours or something?"

"What gave you that impression?" questioned Earle in return.

"Just — just trying to figure out why you only saved those women and children."

"I tried to save more, but, I'm the kids' uncle. Maria, their mother, married my brother; he drank himself to death a few years back. Buried him up on the hill. I feel kinda responsible for them."

"What about the other two? You some kinda ladies' man, Earle?"

"What's with the sudden string of questions, sir?"

"Oh, nothing. Just making idle conversation."

"Well, how about you? Charlotte tells me you're the Sam Hyde Gang, that you came here to rob the town."

"Yep, that we are and that we was."

"So why you now trying to save us?"

"Y'know—" Clayton started through gritted teeth.

"Y'know—" interrupted Sam, "contrary to popular opinion, we ain't as bad as the law makes out to be. Sure, we rob, and I admit we have killed before, but only ever in self-defence. We wanna be free, so, do you think we enjoy adding more fives and zeroes to the ends of our bounties?"

"And if we make it out of this alive, y'all gonna be going back to murdering folk and robbing banks and trains?" asked Earle.

Janie's eyes widened with anger, "I didn't rob no   "

"Let it go, Janie. Let it go," comforted Virgil with a wry smile.

Janie huffed and mumbled a slew of obscenities under her breath as the group neared the mine.

"Once we're in there, try to avoid shooting anything," said Earle, "it should be all right once we get deeper in, but in close quarters it will be loud, and we're gonna want our hearing down there."

"Well, we ain't gonna have much of an option if those things come at out straight away," replied Clayton.

"I know, but try," continued Earle, "oh, and try not to get bit or scratched by one of these things. That's how they turn you into one of them. I saw it happen. It's why I ended up in that bell tower."

Sam stopped in his tracks and grabbed Earle by the arm to stop him too, "So, that's how it happens. That sure would have been some mighty pertinent information before I came up with this plan, mister."

"I told you this was a suicide mission!" Clayton butted in.

Sam rolled his eyes and began marching towards the mine, "alternative plan: don't get bit!"

XI
INTO THE MOUTH OF HELL

Earle grabbed a crowbar off the ground and went over to where they kept some of the dynamite. After jimmying open a crate, he threw the crowbar to the ground and began handing the red-stick bundles at each of the gang members.

"Careful now, they're stable enough but anything excessive can set them off. There should be more in the mines, but just in case we can't get to them, this should be enough to do some damage… just run as fast as you can."

Sam gave a nervous swallow and turned to Janie, "Look, are you sure you wanna—"

"Stop babying me, Sam!" snapped Janie.

"All right, all right," he replied, raising his hands in surrender and backing away, before addressing the entire group, "I wanna blow these freaks up; I wanna stop these things real bad. But, if we can't get them all, we sure as hell make sure they can't get out of this mine ever again, y'hear?"

Earle walked over to a pair of lanterns left by the mine's mouth and pulled a matchbox from his pocket. After lighting the two of them, he handed one to Sam, and kept the other to himself.

"We stick together best we can," said Sam, before handing his lantern to Virgil, "Earle and myself will take the lead. Clayton, you're in the middle. Virgil, Janie, I want you at the back. If things go south, it gives you the best chance of getting out first. No arguments."

Earle made the sign of the cross, took a deep breath, and led the gang into the mine. There was a stillness to the air inside the mine that made it feel thick in the lungs. Dust clung to everyone's skin as they descended deeper. The minutest movement reverberated around them. The silence put everybody on edge.

As they made their way even deeper to the newer sections of the mineshaft, the manmade tunnels trailed off into what seemed like a maze of subterranean caves.

"The explosion happened down here," whispered Earle, pointing his lantern towards one offshoot, "this is where we first encountered those things once we started clearing out the debris. Stay close. We didn't get to figuring out where all these tunnels go off to yet, so, yeah."

"Ah, shit," muttered Clayton.

As they inched their way closer to the site, they heard a dull and constant humming sound permeating the air. It was coming from where they were heading to, but they all felt as if it was more coming from inside their own heads.

They continued on, reaching closer to their destination, all intrigued by the green-blue illumination that now pulsed down the end of the tunnel they were in.

Clayton's anxiousness caused him to reach for his revolver, but Virgil stopped him from pulling it out.

"Not till we need it," he mouthed.

The group made their way around a corner and stopped short; their faces filled with horror and awe.

In front of them was a vast hollow with a single spire in the middle. The spire, speckled with rocks, gave off the pulsing colour, and surrounding the spire stood a group of the creatures they'd not seen before in the horde. Dressed in Spanish garb and armour, and each holding a pike, it was as if they were guarding the spire.

Before the gang could collect themselves, the creatures all turned to face them; their eyes burning bright and their pikes raised in defence.

"That's — that's not good," trembled Sam.

The gang then jumped in fear as the guards spoke as one in deep tones using a language nobody in the group could understand.

They then paused, and began speaking again, this time in another unfamiliar language.

A third time they paused, and then spoke again, "*Hablarás, luego morirás.*"

"That was Spanish, right?" Sam stuttered as he asked

Virgil.

All Virgil could do is nod in fear.

"OK. Er—" Sam began stepping forward, "habla... er... Inglés?"

The guards let out a singular screech that echoed throughout the hollow and then, after yet another pause, they spoke, "You will speak, then you will die."

Sam turned his head to the group and shrugged, "Well, that's... progress, I guess?"

"Speak!" the guards demanded.

"Kinda — kinda feels redundant for me to talk if you've — if you've already decided we're gonna—"

"Speak!" they demanded again, as they slammed the butts of their pikes into the ground.

"What do you want me to say?" Sam screamed back.

While Sam and the Legion-like guards had their back and forth, Clayton nudged Virgil and pointed at the hollow's walls without trying to be too obvious. They looked as if they were melting at first, but as Clayton focused, he realised what he was looking at.

"It's the freaks, they're sliding down!" he said through a hushed shout, "Sam! Sam, be careful, they're—"

A gut-wrenching scream followed by the sound of glass smashing came from behind the gang.

"Abernathy!" cried out Earle, as he turned to see the old town-owner sinking his teeth into Virgil's shoulder.

"No!" howled Sam, as he pulled out his revolver and shot the creature in the head without hesitation.

The guards howled and the bodies of the horde got up and move forward towards the gang. Earle panicked and lit his dynamite, and Clayton snatched it off him and threw it as far as he could into the hollow.

"Grab Virgil! Run!" Sam cried out.

The gang doubled back on themselves, but as they continued on, they saw part of the horde had cut them off from their exit.

"Fuck!" shouted Clayton.

"We'll go this way!" ordered Earle, taking the gang down one of the uncharted tunnels.

"Go! Go—" Sam cried out before being cut off by the explosion in the hollow.

The surrounding earth tremored, and loose stone and gravel fell around them.

"Keep going! Keep going!" Clayton cried out, as he began firing shots at the incoming horde, "open fire at the bastards!"

Sam grabbed Virgil and helped him get to the front as Clayton and Janie continued to shoot.

"C'mon — c'mon old man. You're not — not dying on me yet!" Sam stuttered, feeling Virgil struggling to continue on, "c'mon you ole bastard!"

"Sam—" Virgil tried to speak.

"No, no, no, no," panicked Sam.

Virgil pulled his pocket watch out, yanked it from its chain, and handed it to Sam, "I'm — son — I."

"Virgil! N — no! No!"

The old man's body went limp and slipped out of Sam's grip; he slumped to the floor and convulsed for a moment before becoming lifeless.

"He's gonna turn!" cried out Earle over the gunfire.

"What's going—" Clayton turned to see Virgil's body on the floor, "ah, fuck!"

"No!" screamed Janie as she turned and saw Virgil too.

"I'm so sorry, old man," whispered Sam, as he pulled Virgil's satchel off his body.

"Fuck this!" Clayton cried out as he grabbed the dynamite Virgil tucked into his pants.

He grabbed the matchbox from Earle, lit the stick and threw it into the horde, "Everybody, run!"

Sam grabbed Janie and helped her run farther into the tunnel with Clayton and Earle.

"Stop blowing everything up, Clay—" the explosion stopped Sam short and sent everyone tumbling to the floor.

A low rumble followed by horrendous noises began. Earle recognised the sound in an instant.

"Move! It's a collapse!"

The gang scrambled up and rushed away from the falling debris, which blocked off that part of the cave.

"Shit! Shit, fuck! Fuck! Are you — shit! You shit fuck, fucking shit!" screamed Clayton, stamping his feet and kicking the loose gravel around.

"Clayton!" barked Sam, "if you're quite done airing your lungs?"

"I ain't stopping shit, *boss*!" continued Clayton, "the old man's dead! We're trapped down here! This is all—"

"You shut your damn mouth Clayton H. Starr or so help me God I will—"

"You'll what, Sam, hmm?"

"Will you two quit your piss slinging!" shouted Janie, "fucking Christ almighty!"

"We never got around to traversing this part of the cave system," interrupted Earle.

"So?" huffed Clayton.

"So, it could lead around to another branch. We might be lucky and get a way out, maybe even get around those things and block them in with what dynamite we got left."

Sam rubbed his chin in thought, "Sounds like an awful slim—"

"Fuck it, we got nothing left to lose now, let's just go," interrupted Clayton as he grabbed the lantern from Earle and marched on into the darkness, "better keep up, folks, cause I ain't stopping."

Earle followed Clayton, with Sam keeping Janie at a good pace. They continued to walk deeper and deeper into the cave; it felt to them like it stretched on for an eternity. The uneven terrain soon sloped down into a knee-high pool of water.

"Watch your footing," Earle said to Clayton, "if that lantern gets wet, we're stuck here in the dark."

Clayton continued to huff with frustration and powered through the water.

The ground soon sloped up again, and the gang climbed up the steep incline. As they got higher, they were all hit with a familiar humming sound.

"You can all hear that, right?" Janie asked.

"Yeah," replied the three men.

Panic-stricken, they climbed upwards until the ground levelled out again, but the new tunnel they found themselves in wasn't big enough to stand all the way up in.

"Er — Clayton," said Earle, "turn the lantern off."

"What? You wanna sit in the dark and sing campfire songs till we die of starvation?" barked Clayton.

"No! I think — I think I see something."

"Just do it, Clay," ordered Sam.

"Fine!"

Clayton turned the lantern off, and to everyone's amazement, the cave did not turn pitch black. Further down the cave, the colourful glow of the spire seemed to emanate out of a wall.

"Wait here," whispered Sam, as he crawled his way towards the light.

The humming got louder and the light brighter as he got closer to the source. It was a series of open cracks in the cave wall that opened out into the hollow.

Sam peered through and could see that the trail had led to a position behind the hollow's entrance. He noticed that, unlike the last explosion, the first one did not cause a cave in. Instead, there were just bodies and small boulders spread across the floor.

"*Son of a bitch…*" he said with a grin.

He then noticed how the old Spanish guards had gone back to standing around the spire.

"Why is that spire so damn important?" he asked himself.

Sam then thought to check if the wall was loose enough to turn the cracks into a larger hole. He took great care as he pulled at the rocks, letting them snap off in his hands, and placed the chunks beside him.

After a while, Clayton crawled up behind him, "What the hell are you doing?"

"Shh!" Sam hushed, and then pointed at the hole, "go gather everyone's dynamite."

Clayton rolled his eyes and did as Sam asked, while Sam continued to make the hole large enough for someone to climb through.

Clayton returned with the last of the dynamite and handed it to Sam.

"I got a plan," said Sam, pulling off some fuses and tying them together, "you and me, we're gonna go down there and try to get this bundle as close to that glowing spire they seem to wanna protect."

"We're not making it out of this, are we?" asked Clayton.

"You want my honest answer?" replied Sam, "I doubt it. But if we can make sure these things don't make it out either then I'm happy with that."

"Well, I ain't!" panicked Clayton.

"Look, Clay, we either sit around and starve or we stop this thing from taking more lives. We're outlaws, brother, we're not assholes."

Clayton sighed and tensed his jaw, "All right, so how we gonna do this?"

"Janie. She's the best shot with a rifle. We'll have her perched up here with Mr Miner Forty-Niner," Sam tied the sticks into a bundle with the fuses he'd just fashioned, "you and me, we'll slide down, talk some shit, get them away from the spire. Then we throw the dynamite, find cover, and if the impact don't set it off, then we let Janie take the shot."

"This is a terrible plan, Sam."

"Sure is, Clay. Now go get Janie."

XII
A LAST-DITCH EFFORT

Sam and Clayton took great care as they slid down the wall of the hollow and then walked towards its centre.

"I'm ready to talk now!" Sam boasted.

The guards all turned to face the two men, and at once let out a singular, sharp scream.

"Where are my manners?" said Sam, stepping closer to the spire with Clayton behind him, "my name is Sam Hyde of the Sam Hyde Gang, and this here is my associate, one mister Clayton H. Starr. I don't know what the 'H' stands for, but he assures me it does not stand for Helen, as I once guessed under the influence of a bottle of whiskey many moons ago."

"You will stop, and you will die!" howled the guards in unison.

"Oh, I got no intention of stopping," Sam continued, "though me and my compadre here, we're content with the fact that we're gonna die."

"You will stop—"

"Yeah, yeah, we get it already! Jesus Christ almighty up in Heaven with all the angels and such," shouted Sam, "here's the thing, though… we're outlaws, and we er — we don't go down without a fight."

Sam pulled out his revolvers and began firing at the guards. As predicted, the guards charged towards them. They didn't shuffle like the rest of the horde, and their faster movements took Sam and Clayton by surprise.

They both began firing, desperate for them and the guards to get far enough away from the spire.

"C'mon you bastards!" cried out Clayton.

"Just a little more," shouted Sam, as he tried to make every shot count, "how's that throwing arm, Clay?"

"Only one way to find out!" Clayton shouted, before grabbing the dynamite bundle out from behind Sam's back.

He took a few steps back, cocked his arm, and took a run-up before letting the sticks fly. The dynamite soared through the air, and just as it reached its target, the fusing came loose, and the sticks separated.

"How's your knotting skills, Sam?" mocked Clayton.

"Ah, fuck!" Sam shouted back, "Janie! Janie now!"

"Fuck!" Janie muttered, trying to eye up the dynamite stick closest to the spire.

"Look! The creatures are piling in from the entrance!" exclaimed Earle.

"Damn it!" cried out Janie, "boss! You got more company!"

Sam looked over to see the horde shuffling into the hollow.

"Janie! Take a shot now! Do it!"

"Take the fucking shot!" screamed Clayton, as he tried to calm his frantic shaking and reload his gun.

Janie spotted the stick closest to the spire, took a deep breath, aimed, and squeezed the trigger as she exhaled.

She missed the first shot.

Janie took another deep breath, corrected her aim, and squeezed the trigger again.

Another miss.

"Janie! You got this! Just do it!" screamed Sam.

Janie fired a third shot, but this time at a guard trying to sneak around Clayton.

"The dynamite, woman!" Clayton shouted, "shoot the damn—"

A loud explosion followed by more explosions burst into the air. Plumes of grey-brown smoke filled the centre of the room, and the spire began crumbling. The whole hollow then rocked as the spire toppled down, sending a wave of dirt and debris out like a pond ripple, engulfing Sam, Clayton, and the foul creatures of the horde. As the spire continued to fall, the light from it got dimmer until the hollow became pitch black.

"No!" screamed Janie as tears flooded down her face.

Earle pulled out a match and, with shaking hands, tried to relight the lantern.

The two of them looked on into the darkness, hoping to see any kind of sign from Sam or Clayton.

Five minutes passed, and the dust seemed to settle enough to show that none of the horde survived. No sets of glowing eyes. No dull glow from the spire's remains. Just darkness.

Janie and Earle clambered down and searched with the dimming lantern.

"Sam? Clay?" Janie called out, "boss? Asshole?"

Through the light of the lantern, they saw the horde's bodies disintegrate and leave nothing but their clothes behind.

"Argh!" a voice cried out in the dark.

"Sam?" Janie screamed as she hobbled towards him.

"Jan — Janie? Where — Clay? Clayton!" he coughed out.

"I'm here," Clayton muttered from a few feet away.

Before they could continue, the ground rumbled again.

"We need to leave! Now!" ordered Earle.

He helped Clayton up and the four of them moved as fast as they could towards what they hoped was a way out and not a dead end.

"Go! Go! This way! This way!" Earle barked, as he led them through the caves back into the manmade tunnels.

The hollow collapsed in on itself, causing dust to shoot through and follow the group as they headed upwards towards the bright light of daylight and salvation.

"Just a little further!" cried out Sam.

The sunlight had never felt so good to any of them as it hit their skin. They continued to run until they felt safe, then one by one they all collapsed onto the ground and let out hysterical bouts of laughter.

"Holy shit!" cried out Clayton, "holy shit!"

Sam felt an arm around him as he knelt there shaking. He looked at his shoulder to see Janie's hand resting there. Without saying a word, he held it and whimpered.

"The old man would have been proud of you," she whispered, "hell, for all we know, we just saved the damn world."

Sam's cries got louder, and Janie sat herself in front of him and lifted his head up to face her, "When I joined the gang, Virgil used to read with me to help me read and write better. You remember? There was a book by some Frenchman, and there was a line that always stuck with me. 'My friend, be a man: women weep for the dead, but men revenge them.'"

"I'm not weeping, Janie," smiled Sam, "just — just got some dust in my eyes is all."

"You're such an asshole," she smiled back, before standing up and holding her hand out to help him up.

The group regained their strength and took a moment to let the adrenaline fade. It was long past midday by the time they had energy to walk back into town.

Earle waved his arms with an enormous smile on his face when he saw the glint of the scope from Charlotte's rifle on the roof.

"They're alive!" they heard her shout, "they're alive!"

XIII
EPILOGUE

Three weeks later, the Sam Hyde Gang found themselves in chains, sat in the back of a police wagon, awaiting transfer onto a train to be transported to Yuma Territorial Prison.

"Wonder how long before we're invited to a necktie social?" said Clayton.

"We're just lucky they didn't shoot us on the damn spot when they turned up," said Sam.

"Well, we could have talked our way out of it had that mouthy bitch not blurted out who we were as soon as the cavalry turned up," huffed Janie.

"You didn't help matters!" hissed Clayton.

"I don't—"

"You pulled a gun on her! In front of the United States Army!"

"I—"

"You threatened to cut her damn breasts off!"

"Well—"

Sam gave out a loud sigh, "Enough! Jesus!"

The gate of the wagon's cage opened, "Get your worthless asses out here now. One at a time! Nice and slow!"

"Time to go on holiday, I guess," joked Sam, climbing out at gunpoint.

Janie, Clayton, Onacona and Reuben all followed one by one, and they stood in a line waiting for their next set of orders.

"Right! Move it!" ordered the officer.

"By order of the President of the United States, you will not let those people onto that train!" shouted a man with an English accent, "release them, post-haste!"

The gang looked around at each other in sheer confusion.

The police officer charged up to the stranger, "These criminals? I don't think—"

"These criminals? President Arthur pardoned them himself, and with that, the charged rescinded. They are now under my protection. Here's the relevant paperwork. So, if you would be so kind, release them."

"Now, just wait a minute!"

"Officer! Release these people at once. That is an order, signed by *your* president. Are you defying an order from the president, sir?"

The officer, startled by the stranger's bombardment of words, gave a hesitant signal for the gang's release.

"Thank you, officer. I shall be sure to let the president know of your obedience. This country needs more men like you!" said the Englishman, before turning to the gang, "right, come on now, we have much to discuss."

"Yeah, yeah we do," said Sam, with a nervous curiosity.

"Hezekiah Rackham. How do you do?" the Englishman continued, shaking each member's hand as they walked along.

"What's going on, mister er... Rackham?"

"Let's get out of earshot from these people before we discuss our business, yes?"

The gang, still confused by everything going on, followed the strange Englishman to a nearby saloon with its closed sign up.

"Come, come, come, sit. Please, sit," he said to the gang as he signalled the barman.

The gang sat around a round table in the saloon's corner and watched in silence as the barman came with half a dozen glasses, a bottle of whiskey, and a look of annoyance at Onacona.

"Thank you, barkeep. Now, if you'd be so kind?" said Hezekiah, suggesting to the barman to leave the room.

He took a seat on a rickety chair, settled himself, and looked at the gang. He then pointed at them one by one, "Onacona: the brave Cherokee warrior. Reuben Jacobson: the young runaway Jew. Janie Riley: the Texan huntress. Clayton H. Starr: the former Confederate cavalryman, and Samuel Hyde: the leader of this troupe of vagabonds."

The gang continued to stare back at him in silence.

"I'm sorry for your loss, by the by. One Virgil Blake, yes?"

"You don't get to say his name," growled Clayton.

Sam calmed Clayton down by slinging a glass and the bottle towards him, "What do you want, Mr Rackham?"

"I was on assignment from London and I — I work for a group called The Society. It's all very hush-hush. Anyway, my official title is 'Investigator of all Things Unnatural,' though, more often than not, I am more of an exterminator of sorts."

"You some sorta crazy person, mister?" Janie asked, grabbing her own glass.

"You could say that The Society has many a friend in many a high place," said Hezekiah, ignoring Janie's question, "hence, as soon as I heard about your little adventure, I pulled some strings to get you all pardoned and made my journey down here as quick as possible."

"And what '*little adventure*' would that be?" Sam asked, grabbing a glass for himself.

"The events that transpired in the town of Abernathy in New Mexico Territory last month. Well, last year now, I suppose. I've already interviewed the survivors and pieced together quite the picture."

"Is that so?"

"Yes, quite. So, you faced a most hostile and unnatural force and lived to tell the tale. I find myself rather impressed by your exploits."

"Get to the point, already," muttered Clayton.

Hezekiah coughed in embarrassment and also reached for a glass, "You went into that town with selfish, yet understandable, intentions. Yet, you turned from selfish to selfless, even against your own self interests. So, I'm offering you all a job. This world of ours, there is a hidden strangeness to it that most people couldn't even attempt to dream of. The Society wants to expand into these lands. We have offices dotted around the former colony states but out here... out here there is much that goes on that needs tending to."

The gang continued to stare in silence and take their shots of whiskey.

"You won't be above the law, but you'll have a lot of free rein. We pay well, and every month without fail. If you agree, I will stick around and teach you all I know before you get sent off to perform assignments on your own."

"You want us to become these *Investigators of all Things Unnatural* like you?" asked Sam.

"You've already taken on a large horde of zonbi without even knowing what you were getting into. Imagine what you could do with an armoury of weapons and centuries of knowledge at your disposal?"

"Zonbi?" Reuben spoke up.

"Ah, yes. It's the word we've designated for that form of creature. It comes from an African dialect used by the Haitian slaves."

"I prefer that nun-yun word you had," Reuben whispered to Onacona.

"Nun'Yunu'Wi," Onacona corrected.

"No more bounties on our heads?" Sam asked Hezekiah.

"No more bounties," he replied.

"And we get paid a salary, like an actual job?"

"Six-hundred dollars a month, plus expenses."

"Six-hundred?"

"Correct. Each."

"Each?" Clayton blurted out, spilling his drink down his chin.

Hezekiah looked Sam in the eye, "Is that a yes, then?"

Sam looked around at his gang for approval. Each of them gave a single, silent nod, took a shot of whiskey, and declared, "For Virgil."

"Well then, Mr Rackham," Sam said with a smile, "where do we sign?"

THE SAME HYDE GANG WILL RETURN IN...

THE HUNTING GROUND

ABOUT THE AUTHOR

J. A. Dawson is a nobody that just wanted to write a book. After spending eleven years creating a mythological universe to turn into an epic fifteen book saga, he gave up and instead opted to write a novella set in the American Wild West. Some would argue that this 'About the Author' is a little unprofessional, but J. A. Dawson dislikes writing in the third person because he has low self-esteem and it makes him feel unnaturally pretentious.

He also hopes you enjoyed the book, and that you'll look forward to the next one.

Printed in Great Britain
by Amazon

43900394R00085